Symbols of Our Country

I Visit the Liberty Bell

Whitney Hopper

illustrated by
Aurora Aguilera

press

New York

Published in 2017 by The Rosen Publishing Group, Inc.
29 East 21st Street, New York, NY 10010

First Edition

Managing Editor: Nathalie Beullens-Maoui
Editor: Caitie McAneney
Book Design: Michael Flynn
Illustrator: Aurora Aguilera

Library of Congress Cataloging-in-Publication Data

Names: Hopper, Whitney, author.
Title: I visit the Liberty Bell / Whitney Hopper.
Description: New York : PowerKids Press, [2017] | Series: Symbols of our
  country | Includes index.
Identifiers: LCCN 2016027640| ISBN 9781499427325 (pbk. book) | ISBN
  9781508153085 (6 pack) | ISBN 9781499427332 (library bound book)
Subjects: LCSH: Liberty Bell–Juvenile literature. | Philadelphia
  (Pa.)–Buildings, structures, etc.–Juvenile literature.
Classification: LCC F158.8.I3 H67 2017 | DDC 974.8/11–dc23
LC record available at https://lccn.loc.gov/2016027640

Manufactured in the United States of America

CPSIA Compliance Information: Batch #BW17PK: For Further Information contact Rosen Publishing, New York, New York at 1-800-237-9932

Contents

My family is going on a trip.

We're driving to
Philadelphia, Pennsylvania.

5

Philadelphia is an important city in America's history.

We visit Independence Hall.
Many important meetings
were held here long ago.

9

We see a big bell.
My dad says
it's the Liberty Bell.

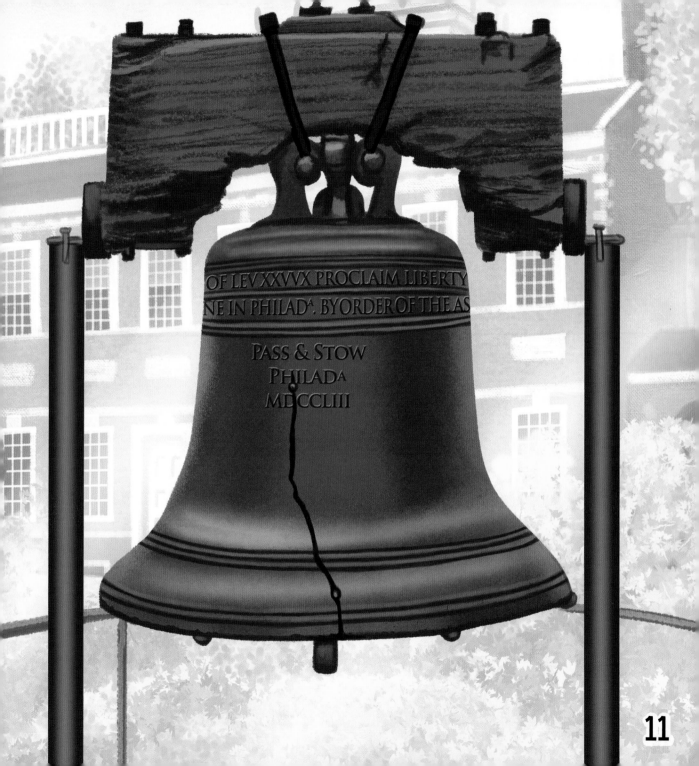

The Liberty Bell is made of metal.
It has a long crack in it.

OF LEV XXVVX PROCLAIM LIBERTY
NE IN PHILADA. BYORDER OF THE AS
PASS & STOW
PHILADA
MDCCLIII

OF LEV XXVVX PROCLAIM LIBERTY

NE IN PHILADᴬ. BY ORDER OF THE AS

PASS & STOW
PHILADᴬ
MDCCLIII

There are words on the bell.

They talk about liberty.
That means freedom.

15

HABITANTS THEREOF LEVXXVX PROCLA

THE STATE HOUSE IN PHYLADA BY ORDER

PASS & STOV
PHILADA
MDCCLIII

My dad knows
a lot about history.

He tells me all about the Liberty Bell.

The Liberty Bell used to be
in the tower of this building.
It rang loudly so
everyone could hear!

19

The bell used to call
people to town meetings.

It also called people
to hear news.

I take lots of
pictures of the
Liberty Bell.

I can't wait to tell my friends about it!

Words to Know

city

crack

Independence Hall

Index